For Jerry and Nancy, my parents

BEACH LANE BOOKS
An imprint of Simon & Schuster Children's Publishing Division
1230 Avenue of the Americas, New York, New York 10020

For information about special discounts for bulk purchases, please contact Simon & Schuster Special Sales at 1-866-506-1949 or business@simonandschuster.com.
The Simon & Schuster Speakers Bureau can bring authors to your live event. For more information or to book an event, contact the Simon & Schuster Speakers Bureau at 1-866-248-3049 or visit our website at www.simonspeakers.com.
Also available in a Beach Lane Books hardcover edition
Book design by Ann Bobco
The text for this book was set in Heatwave.
The illustrations for this book were rendered in black Prismacolor pencil and gouache on Strathmore 2-ply cold press paper.
The display type was hand-lettered by Marla Frazee.
Manufactured in China
0916 SCP
First Beach Lane Books paperback edition November 2016
10 9 8 7 6 5 4 3 2
The Library of Congress has cataloged the hardcover edition as follows:
Frazee, Marla.
The boss baby / Marla Frazee.–1st ed.
p. cm.
Summary: From the moment he arrives, it is obvious that the new baby is boss and he gets whatever he wants, from drinks made-to-order around the clock to his executive gym.
ISBN 978-1-4424-0167-9 (hardcover) – ISBN 978-1-4814-6981-4 (pbk) –
ISBN 978-1-4424-3673-2 (eBook)
[1. Babies–Fiction. 2. Humorous stories.] I. Title.
PZ7.F866Bo 2011
[E]–dc22
2009021991

starring the Boss Baby

AS HIMSELF!

by Marla Frazee

BEACH LANE BOOKS New York London Toronto Sydney New Delhi

From the moment the baby arrived,

it was obvious that he was the boss.

He put Mom and Dad on a round-the-clock schedule, with no time off.

And then he set up his office right smack-dab
in the middle of the house.

He made demands.
Many, many demands.

And he was quite particular.

If things
weren't done
to his immediate
satisfaction,

he had a fit.

He conducted meetings.

Lots

and lots

and *lots* of meetings,

many in the
middle of
the night.

The funky thing was, he never, ever said a single word that made any sense at all.

But that didn't stop him.

As boss, he was entitled to plenty of perks.

There was the lounge.

The spa.

And the executive gym.

There were drinks
made to order,
24/7.

And, of course,
the private jet.

Then one day, all activity ground to a halt.
The boss surveyed his surroundings,
eyeballed his workers, and frowned.

He called a meeting.
His staff did not respond.

He called and called and called. Nothing.

The boss's usual demands were not getting their usual results.

It was time to try something *completely* out of the box.

Ma-ma?
Da-da?

Wow. That worked.

For the first time since his arrival,
the boss baby was pleased.

But only momentarily.

He had to get back to the office ASAP.
There was still a business to run here.

And make no mistake . . .

he was the boss of it.